Izzie: Book Four
HOMECOMING
BUDGE WILSON

**Look for the other Izzie stories
in Our Canadian Girl**

Book One: The Christmas That Almost Wasn't

Book Two: Trongate Fury

Book Three: Patricia's Secret

Izzie: Book Four
HOMECOMING
BUDGE WILSON

PENGUIN
CANADA

PENGUIN CANADA

Published by the Penguin Group

Penguin Group (Canada), 90 Eglinton Avenue East, Suite 700, Toronto, Ontario, Canada M4P 2Y3
(a division of Pearson Canada Inc.)

Penguin Group (USA) Inc., 375 Hudson Street, New York, New York 10014, U.S.A.
Penguin Books Ltd, 80 Strand, London WC2R 0RL, England
Penguin Ireland, 25 St Stephen's Green, Dublin 2, Ireland (a division of Penguin Books Ltd)
Penguin Group (Australia), 250 Camberwell Road, Camberwell, Victoria 3124, Australia
(a division of Pearson Australia Group Pty Ltd)
Penguin Books India Pvt Ltd, 11 Community Centre, Panchsheel Park, New Delhi – 110 017, India
Penguin Group (NZ), cnr Airborne and Rosedale Roads, Albany, Auckland 1310, New Zealand
(a division of Pearson New Zealand Ltd)
Penguin Books (South Africa) (Pty) Ltd, 24 Sturdee Avenue, Rosebank, Johannesburg 2196,
South Africa

Penguin Books Ltd, Registered Offices: 80 Strand, London WC2R 0RL, England

First published 2006

1 2 3 4 5 6 7 8 9 10   (WEB)

Manufactured in Canada.

LIBRARY AND ARCHIVES CANADA CATALOGUING IN PUBLICATION

Wilson, Budge
Izzie, book four : Homecoming / Budge Wilson.

(Our Canadian girl)
Interest age level: 8-12.
ISBN-13: 978-0-14-305449-8
ISBN-10: 0-14-305449-X

1. World War, 1939-1945—Nova Scotia—Juvenile fiction.
I. Title. II. Title: Homecoming. III. Series.

PS8595.I5813I993   2006   jC813'.54   C2006-901883-9

Visit the Penguin Group (Canada) website at **www.penguin.ca**

Special and corporate bulk purchase rates available; please see
www.penguin.ca/corporatesales or call 1-800-399-6858, ext. 477 or 474

For my friend Helen Matheson

"The sea is calm tonight."
MATTHEW ARNOLD

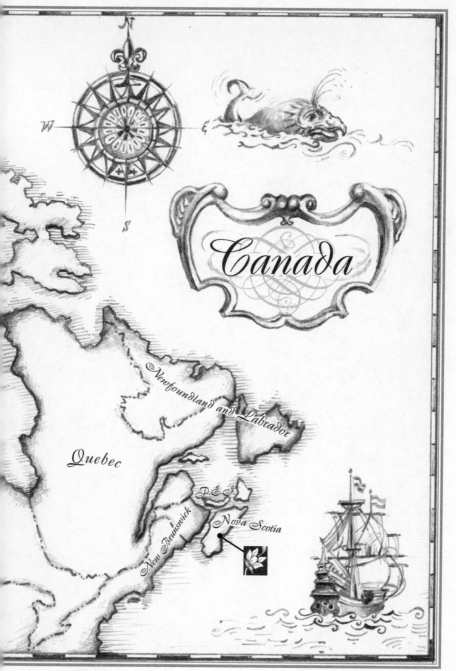

Canada

Quebec

Newfoundland and Labrador

P.E.I.

New Brunswick

Nova Scotia

 Marks the location of the story

IZZIE'S STORY CONCLUDES

I T IS EARLY SPRING OF 1945, and there have been many changes since we last looked in on Izzie Publicover's life. She is now fourteen years old and in Grade Nine at Hawthorne School in Dartmouth. She is also several inches taller, but her frizzy red hair is exactly the same as it has always been. Her father is still in the navy, and her mother has become a respected and skilful secretary at Imperial Oil. Roberta and Patricia remain Izzie's best friends in Woodside, where Izzie's family continues to live with Rosalie.

Like so many young teenagers, Roberta has put on a lot of weight. She worries and talks about this a great deal. During the last three years, Patricia, the English guest child, has shot up from four feet eleven inches to five feet seven inches, and she looks almost elegant and regal with her new height and good posture. She has also become more relaxed and happy since starting a correspondence with her father. Although Izzie has a few curves here and there, she is very recognizable as the Izzie we've always known.

People are tired of gas and food rationing, and weary of hearing tales of death and destruction in Britain and Europe and on the North Atlantic. But by now, the news from Europe is encouraging. The Allies are making dramatic progress as they fight to free countries from Nazi occupation. Canadians are particularly active in their efforts to release Italy and Holland from German domination. It is becoming clear that this war—now well into its sixth year—is not going to last forever. There is a new and welcome sense of optimism throughout the Allied countries.

It is true that, after the bombing of the American naval ships at Pearl Harbor in Hawaii, a whole new war erupted with Japan. But as a result, the Americans are now adding enormous strength to the Allied war effort in Europe. There are strong feelings of hope among the people of Woodside, Dartmouth, and Halifax.

Of course, there is still a lot of fear in the hearts of those who have family members in the armed forces. The war in Europe may be drawing to a close, but it's not yet *over*. Men are still fighting. Bombs are still falling. In spite of the mood of confidence, there remains a very strong possibility that a husband or brother or father may still be killed or terribly wounded before the war ends. And women working as nurses in field hospitals and in other military centres are in as much danger as ever.

Another fear in Canada has resulted from the ongoing spread of infantile paralysis (what we now call polio)—chiefly but not entirely among children. This crippling and often fatal disease has resulted in panic within many families. Most prevalent in warm weather, the illness can nonetheless strike in any season. Parents worry about their children and keep them away from swimming pools and crowded theatres. Some children become early hypochondriacs, fearing that they may have the disease if their heads ache or their legs feel stiff.

But for most people in Nova Scotia, life in 1945 is remarkably like it was in 1942—except that there is a much stronger feeling of optimism in the air.

However, for Izzie, it's not easy to strike a balance between that optimism and the fear she continues to feel. The burning of the *Trongate* has made it harder for her to feel confident about a lot of things.

Izzie and Patricia and Roberta usually met outside the school while waiting for the bus to take them back to Woodside.

Today, Izzie was complaining about their math homework. She sighed. "I hate those math problems. I think there's a hole in my head where the math is supposed to be kept. All I have to do is *read* one of those problems, and my mind sort of shuts off."

"Yeah, maybe," said Roberta, who was a whiz at math, "but you're smarter than the rest of us in other things. Like English. Your compositions sound like stuff out of a real book. I wish I could do that. It's bad enough being fat without being a literary dummy, too. I can't even scan a poem without getting all tangled up."

Patricia was usually good-natured and easy to get along with, and she had been like that ever since she'd made contact with her father, three years ago. But today she seemed cross at everything and everybody. "You're not all that fat, Roberta, and anyway, if you'd stop eating so much, you'd be the same size as the rest of us."

Roberta looked at Patricia and Izzie and sighed. "Don't the two of you ever get hungry?" she wailed. "I don't know what'll happen to me when the war ends and rationing is over, and people start baking gorgeous desserts all the time—coconut cream pies, brownies with piles of frosting and nuts—oh brother!—and when the stores begin to pile up their counters with chocolate bars. I'll be as big as a mountain in three weeks."

"Well," snapped Patricia, "if you are, it'll be your own fault."

"Oh, for goodness sake, Patricia," growled Izzie, "what's making you so fierce today?"

Patricia frowned. "It's all this talk, talk, talk about the war being almost over. And all I can think of is that when this highly convenient war is finished, I'll have to go *home*. Home to my snobby mother in her big English house, where no one's allowed to get angry or sad and where no one's written me a single letter since I arrived at Pier 21 in Halifax in 1941. Home—where I'm not wanted."

Patricia's beautiful posture wilted, and she sat right down by the side of the road on the nearest rock. She looked as though she might cry. "I love England," she said, "and I know it's my own country. But I wish I didn't have such a stiff-necked family to return to. When Granny discovers I have a Canadian accent, she'll have a fit. So will Mummy—if she even notices I'm *there*."

Now it was Izzie's turn to frown. "Well, if they sent you to Canada, what did they expect? Besides, what's so awful about a Canadian accent?"

Roberta cut in, "I know your own accent has faded, but you still sound pretty English to me."

Patricia sighed. "I've been trying hard to sound like a Canadian ever since I was eleven, so that people wouldn't make fun of me; but now I don't know *what* I sound like. So I can't just press a button the minute I enter my house and speak like I used to."

They were on the bus now, watching a convoy move out of the harbour, headed for the North Atlantic. They had seen that sight—sometimes involving seventy-five to a hundred ships—dozens of times, but it never failed to fill Izzie's mind with wonder and a sense of drama. The silence of that huge parade touched all three girls. How could all those enormous ships—destroyers, corvettes, large merchant vessels—move along so quietly, as though navigated by a crew of ghosts? No whistles, no horns, no shouts. A solemn, earnest movement away from the safety of Bedford Basin and the harbour, into the open sea.

Izzie shivered. "I love the convoys, and I hate them. They're so ... *majestic* to watch that sometimes they thrill me. But then I get crazy with fear. After all, my dad could be on one of those corvettes this very minute. And don't think I've forgotten that he was torpedoed three years ago. It could happen again."

Patricia had been spending the summer with the Publicovers in Granite Cove during the time of the torpedoing. She remembered the way those long, anxious days had dragged by, when Izzie's father had been missing.

Roberta put her hand on Izzie's shoulder. "Just keep thinking that the war's probably almost over. Then you won't have to worry about him any more."

"Yeah," said Izzie. "But it's not over *yet*. I won't stop worrying until the minute that happens. He could be killed in the very last hour of the very last day before the war ends. Can you imagine anything worse than *that*?"

They were all silent as the bus drove along.

Izzie wasn't speaking—because she couldn't. The others weren't talking because they didn't know what to say. The thought of the awfulness of someone being killed or maimed *one hour* before the end of the war overwhelmed all three of them. When the bus reached their stop, they got off in silence.

Finally Roberta spoke. "Everything will change for all of us. Patricia will leave. She'll be too far away for us ever to see. She may grow up to be as aristocratic as her fancy grandmother and haughty mother. I hate thinking about that." Roberta was quiet for a moment. Then she went on. "Izzie and Joey and Mrs. Publicover will go back to Granite Cove, and Rosalie will have an empty house again. My dad will lose his job at the ship outfitters, and we'll have to move, too. We don't know where he'll work or how he'll find a new job. And I'll be such a wreck that I'll be comfort-eating and getting fatter by the minute."

By now they'd reached Bessie Logan's little store on the corner of the road leading down to

Roberta's house. "I'm hungry," she said. "I'll treat you all to a five-cent ice cream cone."

By that time, all three girls were feeling in need of comfort. Inside the store, they were quiet while Mrs. Logan scooped up the ice cream. When she handed the cones to them, she said, "Well, girls, today the war news is *very* good. Just think! By this time next month the war could be over!" She was surprised that none of them replied to her cheerful announcement. One of them said, "Thanks, Mrs. Logan," as she closed the door. It was the one with the frizzy red hair. Mrs. Logan shrugged her shoulders and went into the back room to make herself a cup of tea.

CHAPTER N° 2

When Izzie arrived at Rosalie's house, there was no one at home. Joey was playing at a friend's place, and neither her mother nor Rosalie had returned from work yet. She didn't feel like doing her homework; in fact, she almost never felt like doing her homework, unless she had to write a composition or a poem. So she got some potatoes out of the big burlap bag and started to peel them. Before she'd finished the job, Rosalie swooped in through the front door. Rosalie had so much energy that she never just *came* or *went.* She *rushed, raced, danced,* or *skipped*

into or out of any room she was entering or leaving. If it was a dark day (foggy or pouring with rain), her arrival was always like turning on a light in whatever room she came into. Izzie and her family had been living with her ever since they had had to leave Granite Cove, three years ago.

Izzie didn't even give Rosalie time to put away her groceries or to sit down. "OK, Rosalie," she said, with a big frown. "About the war ending and all. How do you feel about it? I know it's wonderful. But me and my friends are feeling a lot of sad things about it, too. How about you?"

Rosalie's dependable smile faded for a moment. Then she said, "I'm actually trying not to think about it too much." Then she added, "Maybe we can talk about it another time. How was school today?"

So Rosalie didn't want to discuss it. Izzie cut the potatoes in half with more of a slam on the cutting board than she usually did.

But Rosalie was all smiles again. "We'll have to eat soon," she said, "because I have an early date tonight. He's a blind date, so I have to look especially gorgeous, being as he's never met me before."

"A *blind* date!" exclaimed Izzie. "If he's blind, how come you have to look extra wonderful?"

Rosalie laughed. "*He's* not blind. A 'blind date' is a person you don't know. Someone else arranges the meeting. Harriet and Alistair O'Connor—my friends from Halifax—think I'll like this man, so they set it up for us. He's in the navy, like your dad. He sounds extra nice, so I'm wanting the evening to go well. Harriet says he's sure to like me a lot, but you just never know. He may like women who are quiet and peaceful and wear clothes that are beige and grey."

"If so, you haven't got a chance." Izzie laughed. Then she added, "What about all your other boyfriends? You seem to have so many. Aren't they enough for you?"

Rosalie was already cutting up the vegetables for a salad. "Well," she said, "they're mostly for fun—for dancing and movies, and picnics in the summertime. They're nearly all in the armed forces, so they come and they go. Mostly they go. They disappear to Europe to fly planes or fight battles, and I never see them again."

"OK then," said Izzie, opening a package of sausages and getting the frying pan out of the cupboard, "if this blind date man likes quiet women who wear grey, he's going to disappear, too. And you won't want him. Wear that red wool dress of yours with the full skirt. Most clothes these days have straight skirts, but that dress will really swing around if you go dancing. And put on those sparkly, dribbly, silver earrings so that they'll fly all over the place if you're jiving."

When Mrs. Publicover came home—late after an extra-long workday—dinner was almost ready. Joey had been there for an hour and was busy reading comics.

"Hard day?" Rosalie asked.

"A long one," said Izzie's mother. "But I enjoyed it."

"Still in love with your typewriter?" asked Izzie.

"Yes. And shorthand is almost more fun. I love my job."

They were all sitting at the table now, and Izzie stopped eating long enough to say to her mother, "When the war's over, how are you going to feel about leaving that job?"

Mrs. Publicover put down her fork and looked at the tablecloth. "I don't know the answer to that question, Izzie. I'll cross that bridge when I get to it. At the moment, I just want your father to get home safe and sound."

Well, it wasn't much of an answer, but Izzie always liked it whenever her mother mentioned wanting her father to return. Sometimes she secretly worried about how much her mother liked and admired Mr. Simmons, her boss at Imperial Oil. And three times she'd overheard Rosalie saying that she was sure he had a crush on Izzie's mother.

If anyone was going to have a crush on her mother, Izzie wanted it to be her dad.

During the meal, there was also talk about infantile paralysis—the disease that seemed most often to strike children, sometimes leaving them paralyzed. Some were even so ill that they were put into iron lungs—huge machines that did their breathing for them.

Usually, there was little mention of the awful disease at home, because the grown-ups didn't want to frighten the children, but Joey was the one who brought up the subject.

"Harry's big sister—Jolene, the one who's sixteen—is real sick. She's had a bad fever all week and a terrible headache. The doctor thinks she might have the Infantile." Lots of people were now calling the disease simply "the Infantile." Joey was looking both excited and scared. "She can't move her right leg, even a little bit."

Mrs. Publicover stopped eating and clenched her hands together in her lap. "Where were you playing this afternoon? Wasn't it at David's house?"

"Yes," Joey said. "But Harry was there. That's how come I know so much about it."

Mrs. Publicover closed her eyes. Izzie felt like closing hers, too. Harry's sister was sixteen. So it wasn't just little kids who got it. She'd even heard that adults could get it. But it hadn't hit anyone they knew in Woodside. Until now. Izzie could feel a new clutch of fear in the centre of her chest.

Mrs. Publicover had returned to eating her dinner, but you could see by the way she was pushing around her sausages that she'd lost her appetite. "Where is Jolene right now?" she asked Joey.

"In the hospital."

Mrs. Publicover looked at the ceiling. "Why on earth," she said, hitting the table with her fist, "did Harry's mother let him play with other kids?" Izzie hadn't often seen her mother so openly angry.

Rosalie—usually so full of movement and excitement—became very calm. "Just think about it, Bess. No one knows how people catch this disease—or why. If you had nine children and one of them caught it, you wouldn't keep the other eight kids home from school."

"Where were you playing, Joey?"

"Outside, Mum. In the vacant lot next door to David's house, playing softball."

Mrs. Publicover took a deep breath and almost smiled.

"We only went in the house once," Joey continued. "To go to the bathroom and to have milk and bread and peanut butter."

Mrs. Publicover closed her eyes again. And Izzie was thinking: *bathrooms; handwashing; passing around and handling food; people licking their fingers and then holding the bat.*

Suddenly Rosalie jumped up. "Sorry to leave you with the dishes, but I'm being picked up in twenty minutes. I'll need every second of that time to make myself overwhelmingly beautiful."

In exactly twenty minutes the doorbell rang, and Izzie opened it to a tall man in a naval rating's uniform. For a split second, she thought it was her father. But this man was almost skinny, with a long face and a big nose. Her father was handsome.

"Is this where Rosalie lives?" he said, with a big smile.

"Yes, it is," said a voice on the stairs, and Rosalie came sailing down in her red dress, with the skirt swinging from side to side.

"I'm Charlie, the O'Connors' friend."

"I'm Rosalie," said Rosalie, "and these are Bess and Izzie and Joey, my very best friends."

Charlie and Rosalie smiled at each other. Then they were out the door, off and away.

"He likes her," said Izzie, *"already."*

"I think so!" Mrs. Publicover grinned.

CHAPTER N.º 3

That evening—quite late—Izzie woke up to hear voices in the kitchen. *Rosalie must have got home after her date, and she and Mum must be telling all sorts of interesting things downstairs.* Izzie leaned over the side of the bed so that she could hear what they were saying through the heat register. For the hundredth time, she thanked her stars that her room was above the kitchen and that the register was right beside her bed. Just like at Granite Cove.

"Did you like him?" Izzie heard her mother say.

"Yes," said Rosalie. Then she added, "Very much."

Then there was a clattering of teacups and the kettle, followed by a short silence. Then the talking started up again right away.

"So I'm feeling happy about that. But what about you, Bess? How do you feel about the war ending? It looks like it might happen any minute. I know that for me, it's both good and awful. I didn't mention it at supper, but I can't stand the thought that all of you will be leaving as soon as Jeff comes back. You're my *family*. It's been three years since I lived in an empty house."

Then Izzie heard her mother speak. "I feel terrible about leaving, too. I can hardly wait for the war to end and for Jeff to get back, but by now, all three of us feel like you're another Publicover. I wish you could come and be the best bookkeeper in the world in Granite Cove—where there are no books to keep."

"What about your job?"

"Well—that's another tough one. Mr. Simmons mentioned last week that he'd like to make me the office manager of his section. This is pretty exciting, and it's hard to believe. But I also know that if they offer me this job, I'll have to say no."

"Boy, oh boy, Bess. You've sure come a long way since the day you brought home that type-writer. Remember how upset you were when I put adhesive tape on all the keys? Mr. Simmons will pass out if you say no. I still think he has a crush on you."

Upstairs, Izzie gritted her teeth. *Rosalie! I wish you'd stop saying that.*

But her mother was talking again. "Well, if he has, too bad. My own man is worth a lot more than that job. And right now, I'm just about demented with fear that he'll get badly wounded—or *killed*—during the little time that's left before the war ends."

There was a pause before Mrs. Publicover continued.

"And just so I can pretty well die of worry, I'm terrified of this infantile paralysis that's hit the whole country. Did you know that three kids in the Woodside school have already got it? Roberta's mother phoned tonight and told me. And they're all in separate grades, with no contact between them. One of them is already in an iron lung. They're like huge, solid cages, with just your head sticking out."

Izzie could hear her mother's voice trembling. *I don't want to hear any more of this.* She covered up the heat register with a towel. Then she crawled into bed and pulled the covers over her head. She might be fourteen years old, but she felt as frightened as if she were seven.

The next day, even in Hawthorne School—where there were no cases—the kids from Woodside could talk of nothing else. Who'd become sick? What were the symptoms? How did anyone get it? Could it happen to me? Where were the kids now—the ones who had got the awful Infantile? Izzie was too scared to want to talk about it. She could see kids actually feeling their foreheads to see if they were hot. Were their necks stiff? Did they find it easy to walk and jump?

When Izzie got home, she wrote a letter to her father.

Dear Dad,

Everyone says the war in Europe is almost finished. I hope that's right. Will you have to go and fight in the Japanese war when this one is over? I sure hope not. I'm praying and praying that the Canadian ships won't be taken halfway across the world to fight in that war. I can't stand to think of it.

And listen, Dad. Please, please, please don't get wounded or killed during this little short time before the war ends.

We're worried about something else, too. Three cases of infantile paralysis have broken out in Joey's school.

Everyone's terrified of getting it—of dying or winding up in an iron lung or having to wear leg braces for the rest of our lives. I hope you're praying that Joey and me don't get it. Or Mum. Mum! What a terrible thought! Pray hard, Dad. For you. For us. For everyone.

    Love,

        Izzie

Mrs. Publicover poked her head in Izzie's door, just as she was finishing her letter.

"Izzie," she said—cheerfully but firmly, maybe even a little bit frantically—"the whole family is nearly crazy with worry about Dad and about infantile paralysis. Joey cried himself to sleep last night, just thinking about it. I've decided to take the last of my gas ration and make a trip to Granite Cove tomorrow. It's Saturday, and it's supposed to be a fine day and almost warm— which doesn't often happen in Nova Scotia in April. You can ask Patricia and Roberta if they'd like to come with us."

Izzie rushed out of the house to search for Patricia and Roberta. A trip like this was the exact right thing to make them all stop thinking about the war and iron lungs.

CHAPTER N°. 4

Rosalie couldn't come to Granite Cove with them. She had an all-day date with Charlie—so skinny, so funny-looking with his big nose, so *nice,* and—according to Rosalie—such a groovy dancer. But Roberta and Patricia could both go. So could Joey's friend David.

Mrs. Publicover packed an extra big basket of food, in case they stayed a long time and needed two meals. Joey—who, at ten, was showing signs of being helpful in the kitchen—buttered the bread and cut the bologna into thin slices. Izzie washed the breakfast dishes and piled up sweaters and jackets and pillows and blankets in the back of the truck.

At 8:45 Patricia appeared at the door with a bag of apples from the Johnstones, and Roberta arrived five minutes later with a box of ginger cookies from her mother. By nine o'clock, Joey and David were settled on the wide seat of the truck, beside Mrs. Publicover. The three girls were propped up on pillows in the back of the truck with blankets over their legs, surrounded by the big basket of food and the stacks of extra clothes—jackets, hats, scarves. After all, sometimes it even *snows* in April in Nova Scotia.

Roberta and Patricia and Izzie had scarcely got settled against the pillows and under the blankets when Roberta started to talk about her fears of getting infantile paralysis.

"Never mind the iron lung thing," she said. "I won't even let my mind *think* about *that*. But I worry about the rest of it all the time. What if even one of my legs won't work? Just think of what I'll look like for the rest of my life: a fat girl, limping in a leg brace. Maybe with a *cane*. Every time I feel hot or cold or tired or a little bit stiff, I'm sure I've got it."

Izzie crawled right out of her warm cocoon of pillows and blankets and turned around—kneeling rather than sitting—and glared at Roberta.

"You just listen to me, Roberta Evans. The main reason we're going on this lovely trip is to make us forget the war and infantile paralysis and all the other things that scare us. If you say one single more word about infantile paralysis or the war or being fat, we'll stop this truck and dump you out. You can hitchhike back home."

Roberta hid her face behind her hands and mumbled, "I'm sorry, Izzie."

"Good!" said Izzie. She gave Roberta a small pat on the shoulder and crawled back under the blankets.

On the ferry, they got out of the truck and looked at all the harbour traffic. The sun shone on the camouflaged hulls of the warships and made them look almost cheerful. Izzie forced herself *not* to think about her father on a ship like one of those, in the middle of a sea that was full of hungry submarines—U-boats. Instead, she kept her eyes on the sparkling water, the rare April sunshine, the wheeling gulls.

It had been almost three years since the Publicovers had driven to Granite Cove. Mrs. Publicover often needed the truck to get her to work or to drive one of them to a doctor or to get groceries. They didn't have enough gas coupons to let them take pleasure trips.

When they rounded the hill and passed Mr. Jollimore's house, Granite Cove was spread out before them. Roberta let out a long breathy "Ohhh!" when she saw the village. The fish stores (what the tourists call fish houses) were unpainted and a silver grey, but the small houses were orange, yellow, bright green, even fire-engine red. In the middle of the cove were seine boats moored to buoys, and the larger vessels seemed even more colourful than the houses. The surface of the water was a brilliant cobalt blue.

Patricia looked at the scene with tears starting to form in her eyes. Izzie saw this and grabbed her arm.

"Listen, Patricia," she said. "*You'll be back.* You'll marry some rich aristocratic man who has more money than he knows what to do with. He'll bring you here and stay for a whole summer."

Then Patricia's tears did spill over. "I'll never be back," she said. "To begin with, I'd never marry one of those aristocratic drips. And if I did, he'd want us to go to some dignified expensive hotel. With waiters in white coats and black bow ties. He wouldn't like it here. He wouldn't care that I love it better than any other place in the world."

Then they suddenly realized that there were two new houses on a hill on the western side of the cove. One was the Eisners' new house. It had taken Mr. Eisner three years to build it, because he did every bit of the work with his own hands. The inside was still not finished, but sometime this summer the Eisners would be able to move in— out of the Publicovers' house and into their own.

But who did the other house belong to? It was big. How could it have been built so quickly? There were curtains in the windows. Someone *lived* there.

Coming along the road, they could see two men. No, they weren't men. They were kids. *Big* kids, *very* big kids, but maybe not much older than the girls.

Izzie brought her fist up to her mouth. "Oh my gosh my gosh my gosh my gosh!" she whispered. "One of them's Jasper! No wonder he hasn't written us for so long, Patricia. He must think he's too big and too old to have pen pals."

Mrs. Publicover parked the truck beside the Government Wharf, and everyone got out. Joey and David ran off in the direction of the little orange schoolhouse, so that Joey could show his friend where he used to go to school. Mrs. Publicover took herself off to do some visiting with her old friends.

The girls stayed by the truck and waited till the two boys came closer—Izzie and Patricia suddenly feeling shy about approaching someone they had known so well. But being eleven and being fourteen are two very different things— especially when you haven't seen each other even once during those three years. Besides, Jasper was with someone they had never met.

Then they stood there—all five of them—just looking at one another for what seemed to Roberta a very long time. She inspected both of the boys very intently. Jasper had black hair and a deeply tanned face. He was very tall, and he had huge hands with long, strong-looking fingers. The other boy was a bit shorter—maybe five feet eight inches—with a tangle of straight blond hair. With his tanned skin and broad features, he was very ... what? *Attractive*. Roberta thought about how she'd like to have a boyfriend.

Jasper looked at Izzie, offered a shy grin, and said, "Hi, Izzie." Then he gazed at Patricia for a long time. "Hi, Patricia," he said—so low that you could hardly hear it.

Izzie couldn't imagine why she was feeling so uncomfortable with someone who used to be her best friend. But he didn't look like anyone who could be her best friend any more. And why was he staring at Patricia for so long and in such a funny way? Also, who was that boy with him? Why did she feel that both of them were different from all the boys she knew at school? Then—in a flash—she thought she had figured it out. It was because they had on shabby work clothes and wore rubber boots. *For Pete's sake, they look like* MEN. *I wonder what we look like to them?*

Finally Izzie found her voice. "OK, Jasper," she said. "Who's your friend?"

Jasper unglued his eyes from Patricia and sort of jumped. "Sorry," he said. "This is Karl Wentzell. He lives in the new house. The green one, beside the Eisners'. They built it last summer. Mr. Wentzell and his five sons."

Five sons. Izzie gasped. But Jasper was still talking. "They moved here from Lunenburg. Karl's father owns the new fish plant in Smith's Harbour. He's my ... best friend." Then he looked very worried.

Izzie laughed. It was a relief to be laughing instead of trying to work out why everything seemed to be so different. "That's OK, Jasper," she said. "We're too old to be jealous about that silly stuff." She grinned at the boys and said, "This is Roberta, and Jasper already knows my other best friend, Patricia."

"I guess you're coming back soon," said Jasper. "When the war's over and your dad gets home. But ...," and here Jasper blushed a deep red, right through his tan, "what about Patricia? Will she live with you again?"

Aha! thought Izzie and watched Jasper very carefully. "No," she said. "She'll be going back to England to her own family."

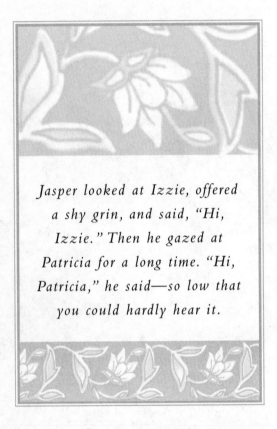

Jasper looked at Izzie, offered a shy grin, and said, "Hi, Izzie." Then he gazed at Patricia for a long time. "Hi, Patricia," he said—so low that you could hardly hear it.

Jasper's smile disappeared from his face, and Izzie would swear later to Patricia that his eyes drooped down at the corners.

"I got a sister about your size," said Karl, looking at Izzie. "She's wishing there was another girl in Granite Cove. Mostly the kids seem to be boys."

"How old is she?" Izzie asked.

"Fourteen," said Karl. "I'm fifteen going on sixteen."

Sixteen. Izzie was surprised to feel her heart do a little hiccup. *What on earth is all this about? I've been with boys all my life. Why is everything suddenly so weird?*

So—what was it? Yes, she'd been right. It was that they looked like men. They had their sleeves rolled up because it was getting warmer—it was half past eleven—and Izzie could see their muscles. So they weren't just hanging around street corners or telling jokes. These boys obviously could chop wood and haul in lobster traps and *work*. She looked at Karl's wide and friendly face, and for the first time in her life wished she didn't wear glasses. And just as she was wondering if her wild bright red curls were an asset or a liability, Karl said—he actually *said*—"I like your hair."

She was so amazed that she didn't know what to say. So she muttered, "Thank you." And then very quickly, "Is your sister's hair yellow, like yours?"

"Yeah," he said. "And straight. All us kids have straight hair. All seven of us."

Seven! And she knew that the Eisners had four.

"Wow!" she said. "The little schoolhouse will be bursting its seams." She'd be sitting in the same room as Karl, five days out of every seven, if they got back to Granite Cove by fall. Suddenly it didn't seem to be so heartbreaking to be leaving Woodside and the harbour and the big city of Halifax.

"They're building a piece on," said Jasper.

"What?" What was he talking about?

"A piece on the school. It needs to be bigger. There's another family moving into old

Mr. Miller's house—he died last winter—and someone said they have five kids. Including twin girls. Lucky Mr. Miller had a big house."

"So it won't be just you and me any more," laughed Izzie. She was surprised to discover how relieved that piece of knowledge made her feel. Not only was Jasper no longer her best friend, but he was also a total stranger. And madly in love with Patricia, looking at her as though he'd never laid eyes on her before. Izzie grinned and did some thinking. *In country places—like here, for instance—people often get married at seventeen. There's lots to smile about. For one thing, there'll be another girl who's my age. And I can look at Karl every day in school.* She watched as a heron lifted off a rock out by Squid Point and flew across the cove. Was there anything more beautiful than a heron in flight? Or any place she'd rather live than right here in this village?

"Hey," she said. "I want to go see Clementine. C'mon Roberta. Come see one of my best friends. Patricia's already met her."

Karl looked puzzled. "Who's Clementine?"

"My cow," said Izzie, "my beloved cow." She was pleased she wasn't ashamed to say that to Karl.

"Let's all go," said Karl. "I'd like to meet a beloved cow." *So he has a sense of humour as well as muscles and a wonderful face. Good.*

"Maybe you'd like to see our new boat," said Jasper to Patricia. "We already know Clementine."

"OK," said Patricia.

"How's your dad?" he asked, as they set off for the Morashes' wharf.

"He's good," said Patricia. Three years ago she would have said, "He's very well, thank you." But not any more. "He writes me every week." And then she gave Jasper a sideways look. "Which is more than can be said for you. And you promised. 'Once a week,' you said. And it only lasted two months."

He grinned and blushed again. "I could promise again," he said, "but I don't write very good."

"That's OK by me. Let's do it. It's fun to get mail."

Izzie heard all of this before they were out of earshot. Then she watched as they walked down the road past the Government Wharf. Jasper already had the rolling gait of a seasoned fisherman—a man who knows how to keep his balance in a boat when the waves are loppy. And Patricia was walking along that road like a duchess: head high, confident, happy. *What a great pair! They're both busy being exactly who they are, and they're a good fit. A strange fit, but good. And she knows how to milk a cow, cook cod tongues and cheeks, and carry water buckets, even though she's the granddaughter of an earl.* Then Izzie's face saddened as she thought about the wedding that could never happen.

"You look so sad, all of a sudden," said Karl. "What are you thinking about?"

"A wedding," said Izzie, before she could think to say something else.

"Funny," he said. "So was I."

Izzie looked at him, and he was grinning at her.

Now what did he mean by that? Izzie pushed the thought out of her head as she went into the barn to greet Clementine. The old familiar barn smells felt so great to her. Clementine's warm body was still comforting to stroke, to hug. Roberta had never been this close to a cow before, but before she left the barn, she was wishing she had a cow of her own.

On the way home, Mrs. Publicover and the boys were doing a lot of talking. Before she slammed the door, Izzie heard her mother say, "I sure know now where I belong." But in the back of the truck—under warm blankets, as the daylight ended and the temperature dropped—the girls were strangely silent. Their time in Granite

Cove had told them a lot of things. Each of them had had an unusual experience, and on this particular night, no one wanted to talk about it. The evening was alive with secrets, with surprises, and with separate forms of longing. But it was going to be a while before each one would be able to work out exactly what she felt. In the meantime, it was best to just lie back and watch the stars in the clear, cold sky.

CHAPTER N° 5

Roberta was even more quiet than usual after the Granite Cove trip. It was as though she were *thinking* all the time and uncertain as to how she felt about the thoughts. But she didn't talk about any of those things.

One day Izzie said to her, "Look, Roberta, I didn't mean for you to shut up about your worries *forever*. We're *all* worried about *something,* and we need to talk about it. I only meant to stop talking about your fears on that *one day*—the day we went to Granite Cove. But that was just our one-time glorious fling. You don't even mention that day. Open up. Say something. My ears are flapping—I'm that eager to hear any bad things you want to share." They were both sitting on the steps of Roberta's veranda, watching a convoy enter Halifax Harbour.

Roberta smiled for the first time in quite a few days. "Well," she began, "yes, I'd like to groan out loud a little bit. I just sort of thought I wasn't allowed to do that any more. I know you're worried about your dad a lot—about him getting awful wounds or even dying before the war ends. That must be *terrible*. But it will all probably work out OK. He'll come sailing home on a ship with about a million other men, and you'll go down to meet him, with everyone yelling and crying for joy, and bands playing. Just think of how wonderful it will be!"

"I've thought about it a thousand times," sighed Izzie. "But that's *then*—when it *happens*. Or *if* it happens. In the meantime, I'm biting my nails down to my knuckles."

But Roberta was on a roll with her own catalogue of complaints.

"Then," she continued, "about five minutes after you do all your cheering and hugging and kissing, you'll get in that truck of yours and disappear right out of my life, living happily ever after in Granite Cove."

"Anything else?" grinned Izzie.

"Yes," said Roberta. "I loved Granite Cove. But meeting Jasper and Karl made me want a boyfriend. Patricia's leaving, too, as soon as her horrible family is ready to receive her. I wish I had a brother or a sister. Even a *dog* might be nice. My dad doesn't even know where he'll be working. I'll be all alone again, probably twenty pounds heavier and trying to recover from a severe case of infantile paralysis. I'm glad the war's ending soon, but really sorry, too."

Izzie had never—in three years—heard Roberta make a speech this long. It was such a huge list of worries and complaints that it almost made Izzie want to laugh. But she held it in.

"Granite Cove isn't very far away," she said. "If you live around here, you can get in your dad's car and drive down to see us. Gas won't be rationed any more. And in one-and-a-half years, you'll have a driver's licence. You're pretty. By then, you'll be as slender as a movie star, because you'll have stopped eating all those peanut butter and jam sandwiches and double-decker ice cream cones. You could marry one of Karl's brothers." Izzie wondered if Roberta noticed that she hadn't suggested Karl as a possible husband. "Or be a big career woman and make a ton of money." Then she smiled and gave Roberta a little squeeze across her shoulders. "Or just stay exactly like you are and be a very good friend to a bunch of people you'll like just as much as Patricia and me."

Roberta had a short little cry and then seemed to be feeling entirely better. "Thanks, Izzie," she said, as Izzie headed for Rosalie's house.

There were two more cases of infantile paralysis that week—this time in Hawthorne School. Roberta wasn't the only one who was afraid she'd get the disease. Izzie had full-fledged nightmares about it as often as twice a week. Her mother wouldn't let her or Joey go to big stores or movies or any places where there might be crowds of people—particularly children. Mrs. Publicover felt as though she were carting around two big loads of worry—one hanging from each shoulder: her fears about her husband on one side and her anxieties about her children's health on the other.

"Will this war *never* end?" she said to Rosalie one night at the start of May, after the kids had gone to bed. But of course Izzie could hear everything through the register. "They keep saying it could happen any minute, but they're still fighting in so many European places that I don't know how they'll be able to sort it all out, even if the Germans decide they want to surrender. And of course the submarines, which don't have anything better to do, are still prowling around, trying to demolish our entire navy. Rosalie, I have a knot in the centre of my stomach that's as big as my fist."

They must have been making tea, because Izzie could hear the pouring of water and the clink of spoons on china saucers.

"Listen, Bess. I have a little something to cheer you up. It won't fix that knot in your stomach, but it might make it a little smaller."

"Anything," said Mrs. Publicover. "Try anything."

"I never, ever told Charlie your last name. You were all just Bess and Izzie and Joey. When I mentioned Jeff *Publicover* the other day, he just about fell over. 'I know him!' he said. 'We were on a ship together for six months, a year ago! What a great seaman! He should have been an officer. He always knew what to do in a crisis and how to make the other men feel good.' Bess. He said all that. Every word. I felt proud to just *know* Jeff. You're *married* to him."

There was a pause. Then Rosalie said, "The Canadians are busy right now, liberating Holland. The Allies are crossing the Rhine into Germany. Bess—we're very close to the end of this war!"

Then Izzie could hear quite a lot of sniffling, followed by some heavy nose-blowing. After that, Izzie heard her mother say, "Thanks, Rosalie. You should be an officer yourself. You always know what to do in a crisis and how to make all your friends feel good."

Izzie got under the covers and did a bit of crying herself, before she fell asleep.

CHAPTER N.º 6

On the following day, May 2, word came that the Germans had surrendered to the Allied Forces in Italy. (Italy had fallen to the Allies in 1943, but the Germans had later occupied their country.) People were leaving their radios on continually, so as not to miss any news about further surrenders in other parts of Europe. Mrs. Publicover had bought a little radio with her last paycheque. She kept it in her office. When the Germans surrendered in Italy, she knew it!

She phoned Izzie at four o'clock and told her. "Why not ask Patricia over for supper?" she suggested. "She's full of worries and sadness right now. She could use some propping up. And having a guest for supper would be a good way to mark the victory in Italy. A little celebration might cheer her up."

By the time Patricia arrived for supper, Rosalie had already made a cake—the first since the last birthday—and decorated it with chocolate frosting. She'd made a little white flag with a Popsicle stick and a white sheet of paper from a scratch pad. She stuck this in the middle of the cake.

"I wanted to draw a frosting-picture of Italy," she said, "but it was too hard. I practised on a piece of bread, but I just couldn't do it. So I decided to make a flag of surrender instead."

"And everyone says," added Izzie, "that in a few days, those flags will be flying all over Europe. Just imagine! What will it be like not having to worry about Dad any more?"

Mrs. Publicover laughed. "It won't be like that," she said. "I was born worrying, and I don't know how to stop. When your father's out fishing,

I worry about him if a big wind comes up. If he's an hour late coming home, I get frantic. Here, if I see a fire engine, I think Rosalie's house is burning down. And if I hear an ambulance siren, I figure it's rushing to some awful accident where Joey and you have been injured." She laughed again. "To be a worrier is an awful affliction."

Patricia was very quiet. She smiled when the cake was brought in but said very little. After Mrs. Publicover's long speech, she did say, "I think it's lovely that you worry about your children. It shows how much you love them."

Everyone knew that Patricia's mother hadn't sent her a single letter since she had left England—just cards with her birthday and Christmas presents. Rosalie quickly changed the subject to Charlie and what time he was picking her up.

"He's coming at seven, so we'd better hurry and get the dishes cleared up. We're going to try to get into a movie tonight. *Spellbound* is playing, and I'm dying to see it. We need to start lining up by seven-thirty at the Capitol, for the nine o'clock show. There'll be hundreds who want to get in, but most of them will be turned away. Halifax is so overstuffed with people."

"Yes," said Mrs. Publicover, "more than twice as many as before the war. This makes it hard for everybody—especially for the thousands of men and women in the armed forces and their families who are away from home."

"Hard for us, too," said Joey. "I'm ten years old and I never once seen a movie or been in a restaurant. The lineups are always too long."

"Yes, it *is* hard," said Mrs. Publicover, "but at least we're *home*. They're not. That makes a big difference. The servicepeople must often feel almost angry at the city."

Izzie smiled to herself. The Publicovers *weren't* home. But Rosalie had made life so pleasant for them that her house had come to seem like home to them.

Mrs. Publicover rose from the table and took her dishes over to the sink. Then she turned around. "Rosalie!" she announced. "Don't you dare touch even one of those dishes! Go make yourself beautiful for Charlie. And be ready to race out the door the minute he arrives. And Izzie, take Patricia up to your room and talk about your homework—or about anything else you might choose."

Then she faced Joey. "Joey, since you're the only man in the house, I'm inviting you to join me in the washing of dishes. I'm in a good mood tonight, but not so good that I want to do the job all by myself."

Joey rolled his eyes to the ceiling, but stood up and started to clear the dishes. "Thanks, Mum," he said, "for the lovely invitation."

Upstairs, Izzie put a blanket over the register. Patricia settled down on the bottom of the bed and leaned her back against the wall. Izzie sat at the head of the bed, against her two pillows. Then she took one of them and threw it to Patricia.

"Thanks," said Patricia and put the pillow behind her back. But that's all she said.

"So …," said Izzie. "How do you feel about the surrender in Italy?"

Patricia produced a wry smile. "Guilty," she said.

"Guilty! How come?"

"Because I don't really want the war to end. So of course I feel guilty—guilty of evil thoughts. What I'd really like would be for the war to go on and on forever, but with no one getting killed or wounded. Everyone a poor shot. Each of the bombs falling in an empty wood or field. All the torpedoes missing their targets."

Then Patricia shut her eyes and leaned her head against the wall.

"Forgive my big fantasy," she said. "Of course I'm glad Italy has been freed. And I hope the war will be over—*everywhere*—and *quickly*. But …," Patricia was silent again.

"But what?"

Patricia sighed. "You know perfectly well *what*," she said. "I don't want to leave Nova Scotia or your family or Rosalie. I don't want to go and live with a mother who doesn't love me, in a house full of chandeliers and silver soup tureens and shiny mahogany tables. I don't like it that my father is shut away in a place where I can't see him. And ..."

"And what?"

"Jasper. Why is he so different all of a sudden? Why do I want to *touch* him? Izzie—I actually wanted to stroke those big muscles on his arms. And he kept looking at me as though ... as though ..."

"As though you were a butterscotch sundae," said Izzie.

Patricia laughed. "Yes," she said. "And I liked him doing that. But when the war's over, I won't be seeing him again. Not ever."

Izzie couldn't think of a thing to say to make Patricia feel better about Jasper. But she had to try to offer *something*. "Well, you can at least go and see your father. And you can keep on writing to him."

"That's the worst part of all," said Patricia. "I can't do either of those things. In England, they think you're about six years old when you're fourteen. I'd never be permitted to go see my father *alone*. And no one would ever, ever *take* me there."

"OK. But you can still write to him. So you'd be no further behind than you are now."

"No I can't. Well ... I can write to *him*. But my mother will intercept my letters from him and I'll never see them. My life ahead looks like a big, black, deep hole. Or a wall—made of steel—that I can't get through." Then Patricia added, "It's terrible to be fourteen. You feel grown up, but you're really still a kid. And you have no *power*. No power over your own life. That doesn't happen until you're eighteen."

Izzie wanted to lift Patricia up out of her despair, but there didn't seem to be any way to do it. Patricia was right. Her life ahead *did* sound like a deep, black hole. Or certainly a wall.

"Is there nothing in your future that looks good?" she asked Patricia. *"Nothing?"*

Patricia squeezed her brows together and thought hard. For several moments, neither of them spoke.

Finally Patricia said, "There *is* something. But it's so far away that it looks almost useless. My grandfather left me some money. I don't know if it's a whole lot, but maybe it is. Or will be. I won't get it till I'm twenty-one. That's *seven years* from now. Seven years is *forever*. So that doesn't take me very far through that steel wall. Or out of the deep, black hole."

"Don't a lot of English kids go to boarding schools? That might be OK. Or at least not *too* awful. Maybe a way to make a dent in that wall."

Patricia smiled for the first time. "It's a ray of hope. But not a very bright one. I'm really shy, Izzie. I know I look proud and confident. I practise looking that way in front of a mirror. I've been doing that ever since I was about seven. I fool a lot of people. But going into one of those high-toned English boarding schools scares me half to death—although it might be better than living at home. At least I could get letters from my father if I were there. Thanks, Izzie. It's a thought I'll hang onto."

Then she added, "I do love England. You need to know that. It's so beautiful. Full of gardens and history and big cathedrals. But I just feel like I don't belong there any more. I want to be in Granite Cove, cooking cod tongues and cheeks and hanging out the laundry." Then she laughed. "Jasper's laundry!" she said.

By the time Patricia left for home that night, she felt a lot better. So did Izzie. She was so busy with Patricia's problems that she forgot her own for a while.

But it was on the following day that the telegram arrived. It effectively blotted out any worries Izzie had about Patricia.

CHAPTER N°7

The telegram came before breakfast. As Rosalie said later, "Before we were even fortified by food." The doorbell rang at seven o'clock, and Mrs. Publicover, still in her nightie, answered it. She was trembling before she even opened the door. People don't ring your doorbell at seven o'clock in the morning just to say hello.

She took the telegram from the man and then sat down at the kitchen table. She held it in her hand without opening it, staring at the opposite wall. When she finally shifted her gaze, she saw the other three just standing there, waiting.

Rosalie was between Joey and Izzie, with her arms around their shoulders.

"I said it would happen," said Mrs. Publicover in a flat voice, speaking as though she were talking in her sleep. "I said he'd die when the war was about five minutes from being over. He'd do it when we were at the very edge of thinking that everything was finally going to be perfect. And that's exactly how I felt last night."

Izzie broke away from Rosalie and stood directly in front of her mother. "Wake up!" she snapped. "Stop saying those awful things! Open the telegram! Just *open* it!"

Mrs. Publicover's head jerked a little, as though she really had been asleep. "Sorry, Izzie," she mumbled, as she struggled to open the envelope. She couldn't seem to do it.

Izzie took a paring knife from the kitchen counter. "Give it to me, Mum," she said. "I'll open it for you." She slit it open with the knife and then handed it back to her mother.

"I said it would happen,"
said Mrs. Publicover in a flat
voice, speaking as though
she were talking in her sleep.

Mrs. Publicover slowly unfolded the telegram and spread it out on the table. She just looked at it, breathing heavily.

"*Mum!*" Izzie exclaimed. "What does it *say*?" She both wanted and didn't want to know.

"He's not dead," said Mrs. Publicover. "I was wrong about that. He's just wounded. He's in a nice safe hospital in Plymouth. He's alive." She was still speaking in a sort of monotone voice that sounded as though she were only half-awake.

"I'm so tired," she said. "I feel like I can't stand up. Rosalie. Will you please call Mr. Simmons and tell him I can't come in to work today? Kids. Put your clothes on and get off to school." She didn't even tell them to eat some breakfast before they went. She kept saying, "He's alive. He's alive."

Joey ran upstairs to get dressed, but Izzie didn't move. Her mother was acting pretty peculiar. There was no way she was going to let her be home alone today.

"I'm not going to school today, Mum," she said. She said it so firmly that it didn't even occur to Mrs. Publicover to argue with her. In fact, not very much seemed to be occurring to her.

On her way upstairs with Rosalie, Izzie said, "She's not even thinking about what might be wrong with him. Doesn't she know that sometimes there are things worse than being dead? Hasn't she thought about blindness, or losing your arms or legs, or being burned as badly as an old matchstick? Those have always been the things that have scared me most of all."

"Did the telegram just say he was wounded? Nothing else? No details?"

Izzie shook her head. "No. It just said, 'More specific information will follow.'"

Rosalie looked as worried as Izzie as they stood in the upstairs hall. Inside Joey's room, they could hear him singing, to the tune of "O Canada": "O, he's alive! Alive! Alive! Alive!"

"And I guess those things haven't occurred to him yet, either," said Izzie. Then she added, "Rosalie. I think I feel a bit of a cry coming on. I could use a hug while I'm doing it. I don't think that crying is what I should be doing when I'm with Mum today."

Then Izzie could feel that lump in her chest move up to her throat, and the tears started to spill over from her eyes. Her lips trembled, and when Rosalie folded her arms around her, she broke into a fit of sobbing, which didn't last long but which made her feel a whole lot better.

"Whew!" gasped Izzie. "Thanks, Rosalie. At least I know I'm not in some sort of trance, like Mum."

"She's just had one shock too many," said Rosalie. "She'll come out of it. I'll zap up here from work at noon to make sure you're both OK. You might give the doctor a call and ask him if it's normal for her to be as stunned as she is."

It seemed like a long day to Izzie. Mrs. Publicover went back to bed and slept for the entire morning. Izzie called the doctor, who didn't seem to be very worried. "Shocks hit different people in different ways," he said. "Just try to keep things quiet and peaceful for her. If the next telegram brings bad news, we'll deal with her reaction then. But if she's asleep, that's probably the best thing for her, right now."

If the next telegram brings bad news. Out loud, Izzie said, "Just what I needed to hear. I'm tired of propping people up. I could use a little propping myself."

When her mother woke up at noon, Izzie heated up some soup and served it to both of them. Rosalie came at twelve-thirty, but there was no change in Mrs. Publicover. She still seemed listless and tired, and never once showed any curiosity about her husband's wounds. Once in a while she'd say, "I'm so glad he's alive," or "He's not going to die, after all." Then she'd sit down on the chesterfield and stare out the front window.

"It's like she doesn't *want* to know what's wrong with him," said Izzie. "Maybe she just shut her brain off that thing she didn't want to know. Can a person do that?"

"I don't know for sure," said Rosalie, "but it seems to me I once heard someone say that you could."

Later on, Patricia came over to the house, and she and Izzie both went up to Izzie's room. News of the telegram had reached Patricia from Joey.

"Izzie," said Patricia, "once upon a time, a long while ago, I said that you just had a sissy war in Canada. Not like in England, where the bombs were dropping. I'm sorry I said those things. You've had a lot of heavy things dropping on your city and family, what with the *Trongate* nearly blowing both cities to bits and your father being missing when we were eleven. And now he's wounded. I asked Joey what your father's injuries were, but he didn't know. Tell me."

"None of us know," said Izzie. "The telegram didn't say."

Patricia's hand flew to her forehead. "I decided that if Joey didn't know, it couldn't be too awfully bad. But not knowing is terrible. How's your mother taking it?"

Izzie produced a wry smile. "She's *not* taking it. It's as though she's escaped to some fairy tale place where all that matters is that he's alive. I can understand wanting that, but I can't figure out how anyone's mind would know how to do it. It's like she needs to be kicked awake."

"Well," said Patricia, "I'm not the one who's going to kick her. She was asleep on the sofa when I walked in the house. But I brought you some cookies. That's what Nova Scotians do when there's trouble. If I'm going to come back and marry Jasper when I'm twenty-one, I'd better start acting like one."

Izzie laughed. It was a good feeling. Then she said, looking out the window, "And here comes another Bluenoser. I can see Roberta headed this way with a big basket. Someone else to prop us up. Maybe we can survive all this after all."

During the next few days, it was hard to keep track of all the news being reported in the newspapers and over the radios. On May 5, just two days after the telegram arrived, surrender documents were drawn up in Holland. Allied victories were reported in Germany and in Russia. There were rumours that Hitler was dead. The air was alive with excitement and hope. The final and unconditional surrender of Nazi Germany was expected to happen at any moment.

But still no word came about Izzie's father. Although she'd not yet returned to work, Mrs. Publicover had begun to cook again and to do laundry. But she was quiet and solemn, and almost never spoke. She still had mentioned nothing about her husband's injuries. On Saturday, Rosalie said to Izzie, "I wonder what it will take to make her snap out of it?"

On the evening of May 6, after Joey had gone to bed, Izzie heard him crying in his room. When she went in to find out what was wrong, he managed to say, "My head hurts, and I'm feeling really yucky. And my neck feels funny. I want Mum."

Izzie ran downstairs and found her mother in the kitchen, idly leafing through a recipe book. "Mum," she said, "I need to talk to you."

Mrs. Publicover turned around and looked at her with the same listless eyes that Izzie had got used to over the last three days. "Yes?" she said.

"Mum. Joey seems to be sick. He says his head and neck hurt. I felt his forehead. It's really hot."

It was as though a light bulb had switched on behind Mrs. Publicover's eyes.

"Oh my dear heavens!" she cried. "Infantile paralysis!" She rushed up the stairs. In a few minutes she was phoning the doctor, begging him to come to the house to examine Joey—even though it was after eight o'clock on a Sunday night. Suddenly she was wide awake and full of a frantic energy. Later, Izzie was to hear her mother say to the doctor, "Thank you for coming. I'm nearly crazy with anxiety about my husband's wounds. And now *this*!"

In spite of her fears for Joey and herself, in spite of her anxiety about her father, Izzie watched all this activity and sighed with relief. "So that's what it took," she said later that evening to Rosalie, when she returned from dancing with Charlie. "At least she's completely alive again."

CHAPTER N⁰ 8

The next day was May 7, and it was one that Izzie would always remember. The morning was misty but calm, and she had a good feeling about it as soon as she looked out the window. Considering that her father was wounded with undisclosed injuries and that Joey might have infantile paralysis, it was strange that she felt like that about the day. But she did.

Izzie threw her coat on over her pyjamas and raced across the field to the edge of the hill behind Roberta's house. From there, she had a good view of Halifax Harbour. George's Island was ghostly but beautiful in the mist, with fresh green grass surrounding the fortifications. A few ships were straggling into the harbour, but none were leaving. "No one's going anywhere," she whispered to the morning wind. "I think I've maybe seen my last convoy."

When she arrived back home, her mother was in the kitchen, measuring coffee into a percolator and slipping two slices of bread into the toaster and closing its doors. "Hi, Izzie," she said—*smiling*.

Izzie grinned back at her. *My mother has returned.* "How's Joey?" she said.

Mrs. Publicover's smile vanished, but she no longer looked as though she were inhabiting another planet. "He's pretty sick," she said, "but the doctor doesn't know yet what's wrong with him. He said he'll run over and check him during his lunch hour. I've called Mr. Simmons and asked him if I can stay home one more day."

"And if he really has the Infantile?" said Izzie.

"Then I'll just up and resign. I'd have to be with him if he was that sick—and do whatever I could to prevent paralysis. If there's anything you *can* do."

Then Mrs. Publicover rubbed the fingers of her right hand back and forth across her temple. "Izzie," she said, "we're going to have to face the fact that we might wind up with two invalids in our house. We maybe can't go back to Granite Cove if your father is too severely wounded. I might have to bring home the necessary dollars to look after all of us. An office manager makes a pretty good salary."

Mrs. Publicover looked very worried, but she looked entirely awake and alert. Izzie's anxieties were enormous. Added to fears about Joey and her father was her own secret and urgent terror that she might catch infantile paralysis from Joey. She had heard of at least one family that had two cases under one roof. But her relief to find a perfectly normal mother in the kitchen this morning was so huge that she was able to shove those anxieties to the back of her brain. "Mum," she said. "Turn on the radio. I've got this feeling ..."

"What feeling?"

"Oh, I dunno. Just a feeling." *Like that this might be the day.* "Sometimes I can sort of see ahead— or behind—to things that other people don't know. Turn it on—eh?"

Mrs. Publicover turned the knob on Rosalie's little red radio. *Izzie was right.* Germany had unconditionally surrendered to the Allies at 2:41 on that very morning—when the Publicovers and Rosalie had all been fast asleep. The information was not yet official, but one reporter had publicized it as a certainty.

Izzie rushed upstairs and got her books ready for school. After a quick breakfast, she joined Roberta and Patricia, who were both waiting for her on the front doorstep. It would feel good to be talking with them about all the things that worried her, as well as the amazing news that the war was over and that her mother had returned to her old self.

She knew—and smiled at the knowledge—that she was leaving Joey in a pair of very capable hands.

When Izzie returned home from school that afternoon, the doctor was just getting into his car outside their door. He drove off before she had a chance to speak to him.

What does that mean? He was to have come at noon. Had he come twice? Was that a good sign or a bad one? She didn't see how it could possibly be good. Everyone at school had been so excited and happy about the war ending. It was hard to find herself back in this place of worry and fear.

But there, in front of her, was the door opening and her mother appearing. She was smiling again. "The doctor came at noon and said he wasn't sure," said Mrs. Publicover. "But he just dropped by a few minutes ago for another check. He's sure, now."

"Mum!" Izzie wasn't certain she could stand the suspense. "What are you *talking* about?"

"Mumps!" cried her mother, actually clapping her hands and laughing. "Joey has the mumps! He's a sick, sick boy, but I don't care! He hasn't got infantile paralysis! The war's over, and Joey has the mumps!"

Izzie had her mother totally back again. Here was the feisty woman who had learned how to touch-type in four months and who had done such good work in her job at Imperial Oil that her boss wanted to make her an office manager—the woman who had been able to cope with an absent husband and even a *missing* husband. Now she was faced with the prospect of dealing with an injured husband—maybe a *severely* injured husband—and yet she could still clap her hands and laugh.

"Mum," Izzie said, as she gave her mother a big hug. "You're doin' OK. You're doing great. Let's stop listening to that stupid old radio that's been bringing us awful news for our three years in Woodside and spend the evening *just being us*. Like we used to, in Granite Cove, where there was no electricity to plug a radio into. Maybe you could play your guitar and I could sing. Joey would hear it and feel better. And if Rosalie and Charlie are around, we could all have a real singsong."

"And do you know what?" said her mother. "Tomorrow is the big, real celebration of the end of the war. They say there'll be a bunch of bands playing, up around the Citadel; and there's sure to be a big parade. Why don't you call Patricia and Roberta and make plans to go over to Halifax tomorrow to join in on all the fun? It'll be a historic day—one that you'll always remember. I'll stay here and watch Joey—and wait for the next telegram. It'll make me feel better to know you and the girls are having a happy time."

Izzie rushed to the phone to call her friends. No wonder she'd felt so great when she woke up this morning. All the pegs seemed to be falling into the right holes.

CHAPTER N° 9

Roberta's father drove the girls to the ferry at about ten o'clock. He and his wife had joined the Publicovers and Rosalie and Charlie in the singsong on the previous evening. It was a late night for all of them, and they were glad to sleep in for a while in the morning.

On the ferry, Izzie looked at all the vessels with mixed feelings. It wouldn't be necessary to have so many warships any more. There'd no longer be any need for them to be out there on the sea, protecting people—and shooting people. That was certainly good. And her father wouldn't be on one of them, risking his life every day. However, Izzie figured that if he had just a tiny little wound, they might make him join the war with Japan, but she pushed that thought right out of her head—along with the fear that it might be a very *big* injury.

But Izzie also knew that she'd be sad to see the zigzagged camouflage paint removed and the ships made grey again. Izzie didn't like anything that was boring, and she figured that grey was a pretty boring colour. Like very dense fog. Like a sunless cloudy sky. Like her grandmother's winter coat.

Roberta was looking happy. Her father had already received a job offer from a company in Halifax. They'd be moving, but just across the harbour. She'd look at the city differently today and try to take in all the details of the part she'd see. After all, it was going to be her home.

Patricia was very quiet, and she was wrinkling her brow in an unfamiliar way.

"What's up?" asked Izzie. "Do you know something we don't know?"

"Yes," said Patricia. "Actually, I think I do. Neither of your two families were listening to the radio last night. But we were. The Johnstones and I."

"So?"

"So the navy let a bunch of their ratings out of barracks and ships last night—thousands of them. They stole a lot of liquor and got drunk. Then— listen to *this!*—they burned a whole tramcar."

"Couldn't anyone stop them?"

"The Halifax police arrived in a patrol wagon, with nine constables, but they couldn't control them. The sailors destroyed the wagon, too. The Johnstones said that maybe it was good that it happened. It would get all that craziness out of their systems so that they could just enjoy today, with its parades and fireworks."

"Wow!" exclaimed Izzie. "If it had to happen, I almost wish I could have seen it. I never in my whole life saw a bunch of people go kind of wild."

Patricia heaved a huge sigh.

"What's wrong?"

"Sometimes," said Patricia, "I think you haven't got any imagination. Or else too much of the wrong kind. I just hope the Johnstones were right and that the men did get all the craziness out of their systems."

"C'mon, Patricia," said Izzie. "The ferry's docking. Don't worry. This is VE Day. *Victory in Europe Day*. If they let some men off the ships, they'll have tons of naval police to keep bad things from happening. Last night was a good warning for them."

"Hurry!" urged Roberta. "I don't want to miss *anything*. I wonder if we'll hear bands playing as soon as we get off the boat?"

When the girls left the ferry, they started the long climb up the steep streets toward the Citadel. The area was certainly crowded with people— civilians, sailors, and a sprinkling of army and air force people. But since the start of the war, down-town Halifax streets had always been full of people. There were a lot of shouts and cheers, and some of the sailors were seated on curbs and doorsteps drinking beer from bottles. The girls couldn't hear any bands playing. But everyone seemed to be in a very good mood.

The mood was catching; Roberta and Izzie could feel the excitement in the city and were happy to be part of it. Patricia still looked serious and concerned. "Let's go up Sackville Street," she said, "and get to the Citadel as soon as we can. That's a good place to have our picnic, and it's where all the bands are going to be playing."

But it wasn't easy to reach Sackville Street. As it got closer to noon, the business and shopping district became more and more packed with people, although all the stores and restaurants were closed. It took the girls a full hour to reach Market Street and the Citadel.

"Where are the bands?" Roberta grumbled, looking around. She was tired. It had been a long climb. "There are supposed to be eight of them."

Above them on the Citadel, and along the street, were women and children—babies wailing, the older ones squabbling and fussing, everyone complaining about the big parade that wasn't happening. And there seemed to be a great many sailors staggering around with bottles in their hands.

"Let's sit down on the grass," said Izzie, "and have our sandwiches. That way we'll at least have a rest and some fuel in our bodies for whatever comes next." Then she added, with growing uneasiness, "Whatever that might be."

CHAPTER N.º 10

As soon as the girls settled on the grass, four sailors lurched up to them, almost falling onto the sloping sides of the Citadel.

"Hi, cuties!" one of them yelled. "Want a drink?" There were bottles sticking up from his knapsack and stuffed under his uniform.

Another put his huge hand on Izzie's head and ruffled her red hair. "Curled carrots!" he announced and shouted with laughter. Izzie was terrified, but she stood up and shouted, "You take your hands off me!"

A third sailor said, "Don't waste your time,

fellas. These are just kids. There are lots of other fine fish to fry. Let's go!" The girls could see the four of them teeter along the hill, stopping in front of three servicewomen and throwing their arms around all three.

As though frozen into the ground, the three girls sat on the grass and forced themselves to eat their sandwiches. All over the slopes of the Citadel were groups of armed forces personnel and some civilians, sitting beside large cases of beer and cartons of rum, drinking, yelling, throwing around empty bottles. Down the steep streets leading to the harbour, the girls could hear the sounds of loud shouting, wild laughter, and breaking glass.

As they watched in horror, crowds of sailors and civilians toiled up the streets leading to the Citadel, carrying more cases of beer and bottles of whiskey.

"The ferry!" gasped Roberta. "How will we ever get back to the ferry?"

"Don't worry, sweetheart!" said a bleary-eyed sailor who had heard her. "I'll carry you!" He grabbed her arm. Roberta screamed and pulled her arm away.

Izzie stood up and said to the other two, "It's OK, Patricia. My imagination has kicked in. It's in full working order. Food or fuel be darned. We've gotta get out of here fast, before it gets any worse. No one could bring a band or a parade into this mess."

But as the girls headed down the hill, squeezing their way through the traffic of people on their way up, they heard other sounds—the raucous noise of large objects hitting plate glass, of bottles being thrown through windows. As they came abreast of Barrington Street, Halifax's main shopping district, they could see it all happening.

They watched as a sailor took a huge pole and rammed it through the window of a jewellery store, while another man, bottle in hand, kicked the door until the latch gave way. Then, crowds of people streamed into the store, picking up fistfuls of rings, watches, chains, and bracelets.

As they went about their rampage, they smashed the glass showcases with their bottles to make the merchandise easier to reach.

The girls stayed pressed against a brick wall on the opposite side of the street, their eyes fixed on the jewellery store. But soon they could see that the same thing was happening all up and down the street. The sound of smashing glass was everywhere, and the shouts of the mob rose even above that. They watched as sailors, men in digni- fied business suits, and young and middle-aged women staggered up the street under the weight of dresses, furs, furniture. One sailor had taken a toboggan out of a sports shop. He was dragging it along, loaded with odd bits of merchandise: cartons of cigarettes, a flower vase, a man's tweed jacket, a toaster. When he got to Sackville Street, he sat down among his treasures and slid down the hill on it—the street being slippery with spilled liquor. A man behind a broken store window was embracing a manikin, kissing her on her plaster lips. A woman was racing along with

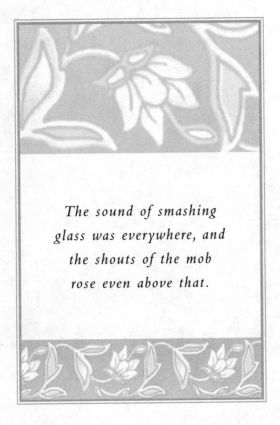

The sound of smashing
glass was everywhere, and
the shouts of the mob
rose even above that.

a baby carriage full of clothes, most of them still on their hangers, a baby under her arm.

But soon, so much broken glass littered the downtown streets that it was hard to walk through it. The girls picked their way through the bottles and garbage and glass and headed down a street that had no stores on it. They made good time until they reached Hollis Street, where another set of shops was being ransacked. A sailor, tall and burly, started to follow them. He stayed very close behind them until they reached Water Street.

Patricia leaned over and whispered in Izzie's ear, "You know what's happening, don't you?"

"Yes," said Izzie, between her teeth. "We only have a couple more blocks to go, but get ready to move *fast*." To Roberta she whispered, "There's a man following us. He's big. Don't look back at him. But be prepared to run."

They turned left on Water Street, headed in the direction of the ferry. The sailor turned left, too. This was the street that held the breweries. On all sides of them, sailors and some civilians were carrying cartons of liquor, swinging bottles to and fro and sometimes just throwing them at the sides of buildings. This was scary, but their largest fear was of the huge sailor who was no more than three feet behind them.

"If I ever get home safe and alive," gasped Roberta, "I'm never going to leave my house again for the rest of my life."

At last, unbelievably, miraculously, they reached the Dartmouth ferry, just as the vessel was docking on the Halifax side. The sailor followed them through the turnstile and took a seat a short distance from them in the cabin.

"Let's go up top," said Patricia. "I want to see what the city looks like from there. And I want to get far away from that sailor."

On the upper deck they couldn't see much, because the buildings hid the streets and the storefronts. They saw that something big—a building probably—was on fire on Barrington Street, but the smoke and flames told them nothing. Both men and women were leaning on the rails, drinking. One sailor was stretched out on a bench, asleep or unconscious.

Patricia shivered, "I have to tell you something."

"What?" Roberta and Izzie spoke together.

"The last three hours," said Patricia, "have been almost as terrifying as an air raid. And the mess it's left behind looks much the same." They were sitting on a bench now, looking out to sea.

Suddenly Izzie nudged Patricia. "Don't look now," she whispered, "but he's up here. The follower. He just arrived up the stairs."

He stopped when he reached their bench and stood facing them. To the girls, he seemed nine feet tall. They didn't dare look at his face.

"Listen, girls," he said. "Don't be scared. I'm following you on purpose. That city was a dangerous place for you to be. You're just kids. It's my fellow sailors who started this whole riot, even though a lot of civilians seem to be joining in. But since it's navy what done it, I figured the navy'd better protect you. My name is Archie."

The girls finally felt brave enough to look him in the eye.

"My dad's a sailor," said Izzie, in a very small voice. Then she added, "He's wounded."

He looked concerned. "Badly?" he asked.

"We don't know yet," said Izzie.

"I sure hope not," said the sailor.

Suddenly Izzie felt she could trust him. "So do I," she said and smiled.

"Something you don't know," said Archie. "I been in Dartmouth, this afternoon. It's almost as bad over there as what you just left. You kids can't walk through that alone. You're only young, but all of you is pretty. You can't be sure what they might try, when they're all likkered up. I seen it happen. A lonely sailor is a sucker for a pretty face."

They were all silent for a few moments. Finally Izzie said, "Thank you, Archie."

"I'll stay right with you until your folks come and collect you. You can phone them from the ferry office. I'll tell them it's an emergency." Then he laughed. "Because it is."

It was Roberta's father who picked them up. Before they parted, Izzie got Archie to write down his address and phone number.

"My mum will want to invite you for dinner," she said. "She makes great fish cakes and the best french-fried potatoes in the world. And as soon as they stop rationing sugar, she can make a truly miraculous blueberry pie. She cans blueberries in August, so we can have them all year long."

"Thanks," said Archie. "I'd sure like to come and have some of her truly miraculous blueberry pie. I bet it's some good."

"Bye," yelled Izzie out the car window. "Thanks for rescuing us."

Twenty minutes later, they were all in their separate houses. Before she left Patricia, Izzie said, "I'm sorry my imagination got blotted out. Or maybe it didn't. Maybe way down deep, I hoped to see a burning tramcar. The same way I wanted our war to be more exciting, until the *Trongate* burned—right on our doorstep!"

Mrs. Publicover hugged Izzie very hard when she came in the door. "We found out about the riots from the radio, and we were almost out of our minds with worry. Rosalie and Charlie even went over to Halifax around one o'clock to see if they could find you. But of course they couldn't. Not in all that mob. They phoned to say they were still looking."

"How's Joey?" asked Izzie, letting her tired body sink into a chair.

"He looks like a squirrel with his cheeks full of nuts. He looks like he has no neck. But he's OK. It's painful, especially to swallow, but the doctor said he'll be as good as new in about ten days."

"And the … telegram? I suppose it didn't come." She wasn't sure she wanted to know.

"I thought you'd never ask," said her mother. "Yes. It came. It's a long story." Mrs. Publicover sighed. "Each time I have a day like the morning when your father enlisted, or when we heard he was missing, or when the telegram came that said he was wounded, I think, 'This is the worst day of my life.' Then along comes another one that's just as bad, like thinking that Joey had infantile paralysis. And sending you girls off to

Halifax—yes, actually *sending* you—and then hearing on the radio that a drunken mob was tearing the city apart. And after that—"

"*Mum!*" wailed Izzie. "I'm *waiting*. What was in the telegram? Just *tell* me."

"I'm trying to," said her mother. "I'm getting to it. As I was saying, just as my anxiety about you reached the highest level of panic, the doorbell rang. I knew what it was. I just knew. It's not like our doorbell never rings in this house. But I knew it was the telegram."

"*Mum!*" Izzie came close to getting up out of her chair and shaking her mother. But she was unbelievably weary. "*Hurry!*"

"OK," said Mrs. Publicover. "I left it upstairs with Joey, but this is what it said. It said there was a big explosion on your dad's ship. It didn't say why. A spark. A short circuit. That's just my guess. They'd have a lot of ammunition on board. But I don't know."

"Never mind the *explosion,* Mum! What happened to *Dad*?"

"He was thrown against one of the big, heavy guns and hit the side of his head."

"Is that *all*? Just a bump on the head?"

"A *huge* bump. He was knocked completely unconscious, and when he didn't wake up, they got him to a hospital as soon as they could."

"Didn't wake up?"

"That's right, and at the time of the first telegram, he still hadn't wakened up. He was in a coma."

"A coma? What's that?"

"I looked it up in Rosalie's encyclopedia. It's when you're unconscious—sometimes for a long, long time. You look like you're asleep, but no one can wake you up."

Izzie felt that old hard ball in her chest again. "Well, *did* he wake up? Is he awake *now*? *Say* something, Mum! *Tell me he woke up!*"

"He did," said Mrs. Publicover. "Apparently he's more or less fine, now, except for one thing."

"And that's …?"

"He's completely deaf on the side of his head where he struck the gun. Completely. He can't hear a single thing in that ear. And they say he never will."

"And the other ear?"

"It's perfect. He could hear the bell buoy off Shark's Shoal if he needed to—so long as he turned his head in the right direction."

Izzie hauled herself out of the chair she was sitting in and went over to the sofa. She eased herself down on it and lay flat. She had never felt so tired in her whole life.

Mrs. Publicover came over and spread Izzie's grandmother's afghan over her. "And what's more, soon he won't be in the navy any more. You can't have a man who only has half his hearing in a big Pacific War with the Japanese. He mightn't be able to hear something that was really important. Like 'There's an enemy ship to starboard,' or 'Steer fast to port. There's a U-boat below us.' You can't have a disabled man in the navy. And that's what he is."

Then Mrs. Publicover shut her eyes and smiled. "It's just about the nicest disability that any sailor could hope to have. He's to be released from active service in several weeks—after he helps out with some work that doesn't require two ears. We can go back to Granite Cove and live happily ever after. The fish won't mind him being deaf, so he can settle right down and be a fisherman again. And if we have something to say to him, we can go and say it on his left side. Not very hard to do. Wouldn't you say, Izzie, that a deaf ear is just about the most beautiful injury a person could have?"

But Izzie didn't answer. It was only half-past five in the afternoon, but she was fast asleep.

CHAPTER N.º 12

Izzie slept from five-thirty on VE Day until seven o'clock the following morning. There was no school again, so after breakfast Izzie sat down and wrote a letter to her father. She had learned from the telegram that there was work that a deaf seaman could do following what they referred to as "the cessation of hostilities"; he wouldn't be able to come home for ten or twelve weeks, or maybe even longer. He was now a petty officer—a fact that was mentioned in the first telegram, but at that time, Mrs. Publicover had been too stunned to notice. The victorious

Allies were glad to have anyone with them who knew how to take charge of difficult situations. There was apparently no danger, but there was a lot of work to be done.

May 9, 1945
Dear Dad,

Happy VE Day, even if this will reach you long after the actual day. I bet you can imagine how happy we are that the war's over and you'll be coming home soon. We're sorry you're deaf in one ear, but we're so relieved that your wound isn't worse that we almost feel like it's a good thing to be a bit deaf.

Me and Roberta and Patricia went to Halifax to see the celebrations on VE Day. Mum thought it would be nice for us to see the parades and fireworks and hear all the bands. Nice! Boy! We were lucky to get out of that city alive.

The army and air force were smart and kept most of their men and women in the places where they were living. But the navy (sorry, Dad) wasn't so smart. They opened up the doors of barracks and ships, and almost ten thousand sailors spilled into the Halifax streets. They were dying to celebrate, but there was no liquor and no food, because all the restaurants and liquor stores were closed. Then the men went bonkers and broke into the liquor stores and breweries and stole almost all the liquor in the city. It seemed like everyone in Halifax was either drunk or crazy.

Soon the sailors (sorry, Dad) began breaking all the store windows and doors, and it seemed like a million people just rushed in and stole everything—clothes, ornaments, jewellery, toys, furs. It wasn't just the navy. It was also some other servicepeople and Halifax citizens and even some kids. I heard one boy yell to his friend that he'd just seen his Sunday school teacher coming out of a jewellery store with his hands full of watches. When the boy saw that, he started to cry. I guess the teacher had been kind of a hero to him. Not any more. He's not going to forget that day in a hurry.

Dad—what makes people act so awful when there's a big mob of them doing the same thing? Does some kind of a <u>craziness</u> hit them? I was in the middle of it all. There was a kind of wild and frantic URGENCY all around us. And a lot of fear, as the bottles kept getting thrown around and as you listened to the racket of glass breaking.

This morning I thought a lot about the day, before I got out of bed. I asked myself, "Izzie Publicover, if you'd been right in front of a jewellery store, and everyone was rushing out with their arms full of precious things, what would you have done if you'd looked down and seen a diamond ring just sitting there on the sidewalk—no more than a foot away? Would you have taken it, Izzie?" Dad, I can't swear I wouldn't have picked it up and put it in my pocket. On the radio today, they said a lot of people were bringing bags of stuff back to the stores, ashamed of what they had done. I guess this is what they mean by "the heat of the moment."

And Dad—the navy (sorry) didn't send out enough naval police to control the men. Then—all the awfulness spread to Dartmouth. It's a wonder we ever got home in one piece—or three pieces! But Archie rescued us.

I'll tell you about Archie in another letter.

One really good thing came out of the day. Yesterday, when Rosalie and Charlie were searching for us in Halifax, Charlie asked Rosalie to marry him—right there on top of the heaps of broken glass and among the yelling looters. Imagine! Not a very romantic setting! But Rosalie says she'd be happy if he'd done it while standing on his head in the city dump. She really loves that man. After all the cartloads of handsome servicemen she's gone out with, she chooses this skinny fella with the long face and the big nose.

Congratulations on being made a petty officer. But we all knew from what Charlie told us that you should have been an officer from the very beginning.

We all love you and want you to hurry up and get home.

xxoo Izzie

Patricia came over to see Izzie in the late afternoon. She was looking stiff and tense. "I didn't want to ring you," she said, "in case you'd received truly frightful news about your father. Blindness was what I feared the most. But your mother says he's fine and described his deafness as a 'lovely wound.'"

Izzie laughed. "Yes," she said. "We all think it's a lovely wound. He can see, walk, and work. You can't ask for much more."

"Well," said Patricia, "I think I could. Ask for much more, I mean. The war is over, and I still haven't received any instructions from my loving and attentive mother. I feel like some kind of valise that someone's left in a railway station through some major error. And no one has troubled to trace it."

Izzie felt sympathetic, but she also noticed that Patricia was speaking more like she had when she arrived in Canada from England, three years ago.

"You still say *valise*," she said.

"Yes," said Patricia, in a thin, strained voice—a voice that Izzie remembered from that same time so long ago. "Mother will force me to speak exactly as *she* does. So I'm starting to work on it before I leave. That will make my transition more bearable. And I'll have to begin a whole psychological transformation. If I feel like crying—which is what I'm feeling at this precise moment—I'll have to practise the fine art of holding it in. If Mother wouldn't permit me to cry when I was eleven, you can imagine how she'll react if she sees me doing it at *fourteen*!"

Then Patricia sat down at the foot of Izzie's bed and cried for a full five minutes. It was a noisy and a wet cry. Izzie put the flat of her hand on Patricia's back and made soothing noises. Joey called out from his bed in the next room, "What's going on?" Izzie's mother came upstairs with a plate of cookies and gave Patricia a hug. But Mrs. Publicover knew that it would take more than a plate of cookies and a hug to take away the misery that Patricia was feeling.

Finally, the storm of crying ceased. "I'll have to find a secret place in our house where I can do that," she said. "A good cry makes you feel so great!" She was speaking again in her Canadian voice. Gone was her rigid posture and her stark expression. She crawled right up onto the bottom of the bed and curled herself into a comfortable knot.

"There!" she said. "I'm pretty much OK now. I just have to figure out a way to continue to be *me* for the seven years that stretch out between now and being twenty-one. To be *me*—instead of Mother's perfect daughter or Granny's faulty granddaughter."

They could hear the phone ringing downstairs. Mrs. Publicover appeared at the bottom of the steps. "Patricia," she called, "that was Mrs. Johnstone on the phone. She said to tell you that a letter just arrived from your father. And she said it had a new return address on the envelope."

Patricia uncurled herself from her position on

the bed with the speed of a coiled spring. "See you later," she yelled, as she flew down the stairs and out the front door.

CHAPTER N° 13

On the evening of the next day, Izzie wrote another letter to her father.

Dear Dad,

I know I wrote to you yesterday, but lots of things have happened since then, so here I am again.

You know all the stuff about Patricia's snobby family, because I wrote you about it as soon as I found out. But that was three years ago. I hope I never meet that cold fish of a mother of hers. I'm afraid I might give her a smack right on her beautiful face.

Do you know that her mother has never sent her one single letter? How about that? And Patricia hasn't heard one word about how she'll get back home, even though everyone has known for <u>weeks</u> that the war was soon going to be over.

But guess what? Yesterday—the day after VE Day!—she got a letter from her father, with a new return address on the envelope. He's out of the penitentiary! He's free! He isn't a bad man, Dad. I never met him, but I <u>know</u> he's a good person from what Patricia has told me. He just did one gigantically stupid thing nine years ago, and he's been paying for it ever since.

And listen to this: He learned to do carpentry in prison. That's what he wants to do now. He wants to be a carpenter. He used to be a janitor. Patricia let me read his letter, and he says that he'd rather spend the rest of his life building things than cleaning up other people's messes.

And two more things. He wants Patricia to come and live with him, as soon as he gets a job. But he doesn't expect that her mother will let that happen.

And he wants to come and live in Canada, because Patricia has told him she'd like to stay here. And also because in Canada we don't care as much if someone has what he calls "a low-class accent." But he doesn't know if Canada will permit an ex-convict to be a Canadian citizen. Why not? Australia was settled by a whole huge bunch of convicts. And they've sure done all right!

You can see that there are a lot of IFs in these wonderful plans. But that's OK. Now Patricia has HOPE, and she's so excited that she has trouble getting to sleep at night.

I hope you don't mind being deaf on one side, and I also hope that your head isn't sore any more.

Love,

Izzie

The very next afternoon, Patricia wrote a letter to her mother, telling her everything that she'd kept secret over the past three years: that she'd been writing to her father ever since the late summer of 1942; that her father had written to her once a week ever since he received her first letter; that now she wanted to live with him as soon as he found a job and a nice place to live. She also said she'd like it best of all if he could come to Canada, because she wanted to stay here for the rest of her life.

Patricia wrote the letter at Izzie's house. "I'd like you to sit beside me while I write this," she said to Izzie. "Otherwise I don't think I'll have the courage to do it. I don't ever remember—not once in my whole life—standing up to my mother. Even now, I know I could never *say* all this to her *face*. So *sit* there, and every so often smile at me, so that I'll remember to be brave."

So that's what they did. It took almost an hour, and Izzie got pretty tired of just *sitting* there, smiling at Patricia every time she looked up.

But finally the letter was finished. Patricia gave it to Izzie to read. "See if it's polite enough. See if the writing's neat enough. If it's not perfect, there's no hope of it working." Patricia sighed. "It probably won't work anyway."

Izzie read it carefully and declared that it was, indeed, a perfect letter. Patricia didn't sound one bit angry. She didn't say a word about her mother not having written a single letter to her in three years. Her handwriting was superb. She sounded like an earl's granddaughter writing to an earl's daughter. Which is exactly what she was. She even remembered to add, "Say a warm hello to Granny," which sounded friendly but dignified. She didn't say, "Give Granny a big hug from me." She knew that Granny wouldn't want one.

Izzie produced an envelope and the right amount of stamps. Then they went out together and took it to the corner mailbox. Izzie wanted to actually see it disappear into the slot. And she saw that happen. As far as she and Patricia were concerned, it was already on a ship, headed for England.

The rest of May passed without any more dramatic events. But Rosalie and Charlie made plans for their wedding in July. It would take place in Granite Cove, and everyone hoped that Izzie's father would have returned by then. When Rosalie wasn't with Charlie, she spent much of her spare time working on her wedding dress. She was making it herself. Clothes during the war had tended to be straight and skimpy, to save fabric. Rosalie's dress would have a circular skirt with enough material in it to reach around the world.

Everyone was busy waiting again. But this time, most of the waiting was for good things to happen. There would be partings, but there were also possibilities for reunions. For most of them, what lay ahead looked good.

For Patricia there were more uncertainties than for the rest of them. The road she was travelling seemed full of potholes, and in the steep places there seemed to be very few guardrails.

It was June 9 before Patricia heard from her mother. As soon as she received the letter, she rushed over to Izzie's house. It was a Saturday, so they had plenty of time to talk.

"Better call Roberta," said Patricia, "and tell her to come over. This may be the most pivotal day of my life, so both of my best friends should hear about it."

Pivotal! Izzie wondered where Patricia had dredged up that word. But she had a pretty clear idea of what it meant.

She knew that a pivot was an object that

something turns on. So Patricia's life must be on the brink of turning somewhere—backward or forward.

When Roberta arrived—fresh from a shower, with her hair still wet—Patricia read the letter aloud to them. It was a very formal letter. She read it in her very best and thickest English accent.

Izzie was astonished by its contents and by the *voice* of the person who had written it. Parts of it became so imbedded in her mind that she would be able to quote whole sections of it to her mother that evening—and to herself, fifteen years later. She couldn't imagine how a mother could write such a letter to her daughter.

Dear Patricia:

I have received your letter, and have noted the opinions and requests that you have put forward.

It seems clear that you have no desire to return to the home where you received such careful nurturing during your formative years. I am shocked that your time in Canada appears to have had an effect upon you that I never would have anticipated. Mother, of course, is as stunned as I am. Why you would prefer to live with your father is quite beyond our comprehension, and your wish to remain in Canada is just as impossible to understand.

I have also received a letter from your father, who seems to know a great deal more about this situation than I do. I have not replied to it, nor do I intend to do so. I have placed the whole matter in the hands of my lawyer, Mr. Henry Hardwicke.

In view of the fact that you have made your wishes and intentions so clear, I have decided to submit to them. I have told Mr. Hardwicke that you may live with your father in whichever country he chooses. I would not expect Canada to welcome a common criminal into its society, but the colonies may have immigration laws that are more lax and less wise than our own.

I have made an excellent marriage since my divorce from your father. My husband is from a distinguished Lincolnshire family, with a very comfortable income.

We shall thus be able to travel a good deal, and with the war over, we intend to make extended visits to many European countries. We shall spend frequent weekends at his country estate in Sussex, enjoying hunting, tennis, and so on; but our principal residence will continue to be with Mother, in the lovely old family home in London—mercifully unharmed by the wartime bombs. We have no children, so we are free to move about as we wish. I mention all this so that you will know what you will be missing.

Mr. Hardwicke will be in touch with you about the arrangements to which I have agreed, in connection with your being in the legal custody of your father. You may address any pertinent questions to him. I append his business address and his phone number.

You may let Mr. Hardwicke know if there are any items of personal property that you would like to retain. I will dispose of everything else (dolls, books, etc.) and will use your bedroom for guests.

Sincerely,

Mother

"So!" declared Patricia, putting the letter down on Izzie's little desk—in fact, slamming it down. "Not one word of real sorrow about my preferences—just shock at my bad judgment. No apology for three years of silence. No regret about *disposing* of all my belongings. The word 'love' is not used once—even at the end of the letter. *'Sincerely'!* I just bet!" Patricia was sounding more Canadian every minute. "Now, at last, she—and the new and distinguished husband—will be free to do absolutely anything they want to do with their lives—without the impediment of a fourteen-year-old daughter with a Canadian accent, who is inclined to get angry and cry from time to time."

Patricia now sat there with her hands in her lap, looking serious but serene. "I will write Mr. Hardwicke and ask him to send my two favourite dolls and one bear, as well as all my books. The new husband can pay for the postage with his comfortable income."

Then Patricia looked at her two friends and smiled. "So now my mother is free—but so am I.

And so is my father. I don't know where I'll end up. It may be in Canada or it may be in England. My mother may be right about Canada not allowing ex-convicts into the country. And it may take a while for us to find out if that's true. But that's fine. I'm not in limbo any more. I know that what's ahead is good, even if I don't know exactly what it is."

Then Izzie spoke up. "And you can stay with us in Granite Cove until you find out where you'll be living. Your little cot is probably still in my bedroom. I don't even have to ask Mum if that's OK. I heard her say once that she loved having two daughters. That was when you stayed with us for two months in Granite Cove, three years ago."

"It seems pretty OK for all of us," said Roberta. "There are a lot of question marks ahead, but most of it looks fine. All I have to do now is lose some weight, and then everything will be close to perfect."

CHAPTER 15

Izzie's father returned to Canada on the huge ship RMS *Queen Elizabeth* in November of 1945—three months after Rosalie had married Charlie and moved to his home in Newfoundland.

By that time, Roberta was settled in Halifax with her mother and father. She came down to Pier 21 with Izzie and her family to meet Petty Officer Jeffrey Publicover when he returned to his country and his family.

Patricia had gone back to England in September to live with her father. He was awaiting the certificates and documents that would allow them to immigrate to Canada sometime in 1946—or so they hoped. In the meantime, he had a job as a carpenter, and they lived in a small apartment in the town of Watford. Patricia's letters sounded very happy, but she was also feeling some home-sickness for Izzie and Roberta and Nova Scotia—and for Jasper, of whom she'd become even fonder during the summer of '45.

Patricia reported that her father was just as kind, just as considerate as she had remembered him to be. It made her wonder how she'd survived during the eleven long years when she'd lived in the icy cold atmosphere of her grandmother's stately home. She also said that her father was "very handsome and a good cook." She had made cheerful red curtains for their windows and cushion covers for the sofa in their tiny living room, using a second-hand sewing machine that her father had bought for her at a flea market.

So two special friends were absent when Mrs. Publicover drove the truck down to Point

Pleasant Park, so that they could see the huge vessel appear on the horizon off Halifax Harbour. As it came closer and closer, and as it grew bigger and bigger, the Publicovers and Roberta became strangely silent. After all the months and years of waiting and fear, it was difficult for them to believe that Mr. Publicover—Petty Officer Publicover—was actually on that ship.

When the boat came abreast of the far end of McNabs Island, Mrs. Publicover turned the truck around and drove the short distance to Pier 21. They all wanted to be close to the water when the *Queen Elizabeth* docked at the pier.

As the ship nudged itself into position at the dock, a band was playing, people were clapping and cheering, and the shouts from the hundreds of men on the boat were deafening. The ship looked like a giant anthill covered with ants; but no anthill was ever that noisy.

Later, Izzie would never be able to remember what the weather had been like on that day, while the boat was unloading. If it had been raining, she probably would have remembered, because the rain would have smeared her glasses and made it difficult to see the ship with its amazing cargo of human beings—waving, laughing, crying, calling out to the waiting crowd. Weather didn't matter. The only thing that mattered was that her father was on that vessel and that when he stepped onto the pier, he would be home to stay. No more telegrams, no more shocks, no more waiting, no more nightmares.

After what seemed like a very long time, the men started to move off the ship's deck and onto the gangplank, and then down to their level. Then there was such hugging and kissing and crying as Izzie had never witnessed. Most of the men were soldiers, but her father had been sent home early—"released from active service" because of a small complication in his damaged ear that made further duty impossible—so he came on the same boat. Izzie wondered if most navy men would have returned on their own ships—the war with Japan having ended in August.

At last they were able to find him in that mass of noisy human beings—a spot of navy blue amid a sea of khaki. And in a uniform that they'd never seen before. That came as a surprise to all four of them. They were used to the bell-bottom trousers and middy of a naval rating, and they had forgotten that his promotion would involve a different uniform. Izzie felt a strange mixture of regret and pride when she saw him step onto the gangplank. She had loved that "sailor suit." But she knew that the new uniform signified that her dad had been recognized as unusually worthy and deserving of a higher rank. So there he was—an officer! Her *father*!

Then everything was a confusion of greetings and hugs and questions and answers. The noise was ferocious but marvellous. The family and Roberta clung to one another until it was almost difficult to breathe. When they broke apart, it was clear that all of them in that embrace had been crying—even Roberta. When they recognized this—the red eyes, the wet faces, the shiny noses—all of them laughed.

At one point, Izzie said to her father, "This is the best day of our lives, Dad." He didn't answer her. He just looked straight ahead, without even smiling a reply. She would have expected him to say something like "Mine too," or "Thank you, sweetheart." He said nothing, and for a brief moment, Izzie felt hurt. But then she realized: *I'm on his wrong side.* She moved over to his other side and said, "Dad. This is the best day of our lives."

"Thank you, sweetheart," he said. "Mine too."

After a long wait for the men to complete what Mrs. Publicover called "the paper end of their voyage"—when they'd finished filling out forms and signing documents—and after they'd dropped off Roberta at her house, they headed for home, for Granite Cove.

Izzie would always remember the view that greeted them as the truck rounded the curve beside Mr. Jollimore's house and they saw the

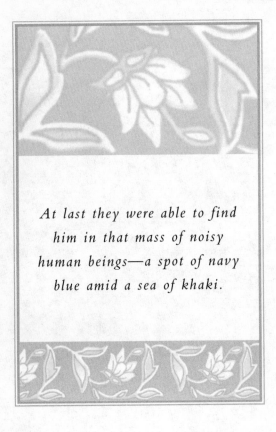

At last they were able to find him in that mass of noisy human beings—a spot of navy blue amid a sea of khaki.

Cove. The sun was low in the sky, casting a golden light on the white houses and mellowing the colour of the others. The clouds were picking up the light, and Izzie knew that in an hour or so, there would be a sunset beautiful enough to mark this perfect day. The grey of the fish houses and wharves glowed in the sunlight, and the water of the cove was flat oil calm. No one seemed to be outside the homes, but as they drew closer to their house, they saw Jasper and Karl walking along the side of the road. They yelled, "Welcome home!" as the truck headed for its own driveway. Izzie knew where the boys were going: they were going to the Publicovers'. There had to be a reason why the yards and boats and wharves were all empty. She just bet that they'd open the door of their house, and a crowd of friends would shout, "Surprise!" or "Welcome back!"

Three years ago, when the Cove people had discovered that Izzie's father was missing, they'd brought food and special treats. Izzie remem-bered that Patricia had said, "Do the people around here always do this when there's trouble?" and Izzie had said, "Yes, they do." *But they also do it at times of celebration and joy.* Or so Izzie thought.

And she was absolutely right.

Acknowledgements

I would like to thank the following people for their help with the four Izzie books: Gladys Meisner, who lived in a fishing village during World War II and was generous with her vivid descriptions of what it was like to live at that time and in that place; Joan Tregunno, who was able to tell me about life in Woodside in 1942 and who lived in Roberta's house; Marie Davis and Monika Sormova, who turned my handwritten texts into readable manuscripts; Barbara Berson, Helen Reeves, Catherine Marjoribanks, Dawn Hunter, Catherine Dorton, and Eliza Marciniak, my sensitive and skilful editors; my agent, Leona Trainer, who led me to Izzie in the first place; Heather Collins, who created the lively illustrations; Jack MacCormack, veteran of World War II, who provided valuable military data; and Alan, my husband, who often supplied historical information and who also cooked the evening meals!

Dear Reader,

*This has been the fourth and final book about Izzie.
We hope you've enjoyed meeting and getting to know
her as much as we have enjoyed bringing her—and
her wonderful story—to you.*

*Although Izzie's tale is told, there are still eleven
more terrific girls to read about, whose exciting
adventures take place in Canada's past—girls just
like you. So do keep on reading!*

*And please—don't forget to keep in touch! We love
receiving your incredible letters telling us about your
favourite stories and which girls you like best. And
thank you for telling us about the stories you would
like to read! There are so many remarkable stories
in Canadian history. It seems that wherever we live,
great stories live too, in our towns and cities, on our
rivers and mountains. We hope that* Our Canadian
Girl *captures the richness of that past.*

*Sincerely,
Barbara Berson
Editor*

Canada's

1608
Samuel de
Champlain
establishes
the first
fortified
trading post
at Quebec.

1759
The British
defeat the
French in
the Battle
of the
Plains of
Abraham.

1812
The United
States
declares war
against
Canada.

1845
The expedition of
Sir John Franklin
to the Arctic ends
when the ship is
frozen in the pack
ice; the fate of its
crew remains a
mystery.

1869
Louis Riel
leads his
Metis
followers in
the Red
River
Rebellion.

1871
British
Columbia
joins
Canada.

1755
The British
expel the
entire French
population
of Acadia
(today's
Maritime
provinces),
sending
them into
exile.

1776
The 13
Colonies
revolt
against
Britain, and
the Loyalists
flee to
Canada.

1783
Rachel

1837
Calling for
responsible
government, the
Patriotes, following
Louis-Joseph
Papineau, rebel in
Lower Canada;
William Lyon
Mackenzie leads the
uprising in Upper
Canada.

1867
New
Brunswick,
Nova Scotia,
and the United
Province of
Canada come
together in
Confederation
to form the
Dominion of
Canada.

1870
Manitoba joins
Canada. The
Northwest
Territories
become an
official
territory of
Canada.

1870
Angelique

Timeline

1885
At Craigellachie, British Columbia, the last spike is driven to complete the building of the Canadian Pacific Railway.

1898
The Yukon Territory becomes an official territory of Canada.

1914
Britain declares war on Germany, and Canada, because of its ties to Britain, is at war too.

1918
As a result of the Wartime Elections Act, the women of Canada are given the right to vote in federal elections.

1945
World War II ends conclusively with the dropping of atomic bombs on Hiroshima and Nagasaki.

1873
Prince Edward Island joins Canada.

1896
Gold is discovered on Bonanza Creek, a tributary of the Klondike River.

1905
Alberta and Saskatchewan join Canada.

1917
In the Halifax harbour, two ships collide, causing an explosion that leaves more than 1,600 dead and 9,000 injured.

1939
Canada declares war on Germany seven days after war is declared by Britain and France.

1949
Newfoundland, under the leadership of Joey Smallwood, joins Canada.

1945
Izzie

1947
Margit

They're dreamers
and schemers.

They're sisters,
daughters, and friends.

Sometimes, they're
even heroes.

Meet all the Our Canadian Girls
at www.ourcanadiangirl.ca

Angelique

Elizabeth

Ellen

Emily

Izzie

Keeley

Lisa

Margit

Marie-Claire

Millie

Penelope

Rachel

Penguin Group (Canada)